STECK-VAUGHN

PAIR-IT BOOKS™

A Fishy Story

Written by Richard Leslie
Illustrated by Rick Garcia

STECK-VAUGHN®
C O M P A N Y

A Division of Harcourt Brace & Company

On Monday I dreamed I caught a fish.
It was as big as a bird.

On Tuesday I dreamed I caught a fish.
It was as big as a cat.

On Wednesday I dreamed I caught a fish.
It was as big as a dog.

On Thursday I dreamed I caught a fish.
It was as big as a man.

On Friday I dreamed I caught a fish.
It was as big as a horse.

On Saturday I dreamed I caught a fish.
It was as big as a whale.

On Sunday I really went fishing.
I caught a little, tiny fish.